So Pucked Up

Up

Thin Ice #1

Charity Parkerson

COPYRIGHT

or encourage electronic piracy of copy-righted materials. Brief passages may be quoted for review purposes if credit is given to the copyright holder. Your support of the author's rights is appreciated. Any resemblances to person(s) living or dead, is completely coincidental. All items contained within this novel are products of the author's imagination.

—Warning: This book is intended for readers over the age of 18. Some of my books contain allusions to past abuse and trauma.

All rights reserved.

Contents

Introduction

Hockey is all Jay knows. It's all he loves. Then he met Callan.

Jay's career has always been everything to him. He's sacrificed his entire life to make his dreams of fame come true. Now that he's on top, he's enjoyed more than his fair share of the one-night benefits. Women come all too easily to him. Never in a million years does he dream he'll get brought to his knees. That's why the last thing he expects is a man to be the one who ends up making him insane, especially since he's straight.

While Callan's twin Cato has always been the star of the family, he hasn't left Callan behind. Where Cato goes, Callan is along for the ride. But whereas Cato enjoys the limelight, Callan is horribly shy. He tries staying out of the way. The last thing he wants is to hurt Cato's career by everyone learning about his gay twin. Not to mention, he doesn't want the attention. That is until he meets Cato's teammate, Jay. He wouldn't mind a little of Jay's time.

So Pucked Up is the first in Charity Parkerson's Thin Ice series. These are sports bi-awakenings and steamy romances meant to heat up your day.

Chapter One

COLD SHREDDED ICE HIT Jay's face, kicked up by an opponent's skates. Adrenaline pumped through Jay's veins as another fight broke out. As usual, Jay was in the center of it all. With the guy's sweater held in one hand, Jay threw punches with the other. At least two made a good connection. He would feel it later, but at the moment, he experienced nothing but the exhilaration. This was his dream. He was a master shit starter. Every team needed one. It kept the opposing team on their toes.

"Fuck you, Ames."

Jay chuckled at the profanity slung his way. "Maybe stop skating like this is the goddamn youth league. My twelve-year-old cousin hits harder than you and she's a girl."

Haynes tried lunging for him again.

A referee jumped between them. "Both players. Two minutes."

Jay smirked and skated to the penalty box. The sound of the roaring crowd kept his blood pumping. This team was his life. His two minutes felt like a lifetime before he was back on the ice. As always, for him, the night flew. They won by one. The cheers of the fans still rang in his ears, even after he showered and changed.

His teammate Cato dressed nearby. When they had been on their entry-level contracts, they had always been paired to share a room on away games. Jay considered him one of his only true friends.

"Hey. Cato."

Cato looked his way. His blue eyes locked on Jay. "What's up?"

"Do you want to grab something to eat?" Jay was still too hyped to go home to an empty house.

"I told my brother we'd grab something after the game."

A smile snapped to Jay's lips. "The twin? Yes! I've always wanted to meet him. Can

I tag along?" Jay jogged around him like a little kid who'd had too much candy.

Cato looked away, making Jay wonder if he tried hiding his reaction. He almost backpedaled. Jay didn't want to intrude. Cato's gaze swung his way again. Something flashed in his eyes. "Do you plan to wear the rainbow jersey this Pride night? Since they've made it optional, I mean."

The question caught Jay off guard. "Of course. Public support matters. Plus, I look badass in rainbows."

A smile exploded across Cato's face. "You really do. Come meet my brother."

Even though he was confused as fuck, Jay still bounced in place. "Yes! It's about damn time. I get to meet the brother," Jay sang as he skipped from the locker room. Cato had been born and raised in

Tennessee. When he had been picked up by the Ice Rockets in California, he had brought his twin with him. Jay and he had both been picked up at the same time. That was five years ago and still Jay had never met this mysterious twin. It was almost as if Cato kept him hidden.

"So, do we need to pick him up, or did you have plans to meet somewhere?"

Cato still looked uncomfortable. "He came to tonight's game."

"Oh. I guess we'd better hurry, then." Jay linked his arm through Cato's and dragged him toward the door. He always lived by the motto: if people didn't question his sexuality with his friends, were they really even his friends?

Cato laughed at his enthusiasm. He didn't pull away from Jay's hold. "I know you're a golden retriever, but don't jump too much. Callan is painfully shy. That's one reason I don't force him to meet everyone."

Jay gasped as obnoxiously as he could. "I don't jump on people. You should know that by now. I'm completely housebroken."

"Mhmm." Cato didn't sound convinced, but he looked amused.

Jay wasn't concerned. "You'll see. He'll love me."

They headed for the parking garage. It had mostly cleared out for the night. Cato's massive black Hummer came into view. A tiny blond with a sweater draped over his arm waited by the driver's side door. Jay blinked in confusion. The guy looked nothing like Cato. They had the same hair color, but that was it. The closer they came, the harder Jay's heart pounded. He couldn't explain his reaction.

"I found a stray," Cato called out before they reached Callan.

Callan's light blue gaze shot Jay's way before quickly darting away again. He shifted from foot to foot. "Okay." His voice came out quietly, as if he expected the worst.

Cato motioned Jay's way. "This is my friend Jay. Jay, this is my twin, Callan."

Jay stuck his hand out for Callan to shake. "It's nice to meet you. I've been hearing about you for years."

Callan's gaze questioningly moved to Cato before shifting back to Jay. He gently took Jay's hand and shook before quickly pulling away again. "It's nice to meet you too."

Jay was straight, but the guy was beautiful. Stunning. He likely stopped traffic everywhere he went. Jay couldn't tear his gaze away from him. Everything about him mesmerized Jay, from his slight frame to his amazing lips. He could dominate the cover of any magazine.

"Jay is going to join us for dinner."

"If that's okay," Jay chimed in, just in case Callan didn't want him there.

Callan looked between them. "Okay."

Cato looked nervous as hell, making Jay wonder if he truly thought Jay couldn't behave. He wouldn't scare the guy. Yet Jay still couldn't stop staring at him for reasons unknown. His gaze simply refused to budge.

Callan cleared his throat. "I hope Urban Mixer is okay. It's not owned by Urban any longer, but I still love the place."

Jay shrugged. "Sure. I've never actually eaten there, but I'm game."

To his surprise, Callan lit a hair. He seemed to peek from his shell just a bit. "Really? It's amazing. Even if you don't enjoy the food, the restaurant is an experience."

He had Jay's attention. "Sounds great. Do you guys want me to meet you there, or would you like to ride with me?" He honestly didn't want to give up Callan's company.

Callan's gaze darted toward Cato, as if he needed his brother to decide.

Cato rubbed the back of his neck. "Um. Why don't you follow us there? That way, you're not trapped in case you want to leave early."

A bright smile snapped to Jay's lips as an idea struck. "Excellent." He stepped Callan's way and draped his arm across the guy's shoulders before he could scurry away from him. "Callan will ride with me. It's past time for him to spill all your secrets."

Cato's expression went two steps beyond horrified. Jay honestly didn't understand what in the hell was happening. Cato had been his friend for years. Surely, he didn't honestly think Jay would harm his brother.

"It's okay," Callan said, sounding shy but firm.

Cato blinked, obviously surprised by Callan's reassurance. "Are you sure?"

Callan peeked up at Jay before meeting his twin's stare again. "Yeah. I'll be fine."

With one last look between them, Cato shrugged. "All right. I'll see you two there." He climbed into his vehicle, leaving Callan to Jay's clutches. Now Jay just had to figure out what in the hell he wanted so badly from the guy.

Callan was a nervous wreck. There was no other way to put things. He couldn't stop twisting his fingers. His gaze kept sliding Jay's way. He was huge. Callan couldn't explain why he had agreed to ride with Jay. Maybe it was the way Jay put his arm across his shoulders. His arm was massive—like he was rock solid. Yet he hadn't burdened Callan with the weight of his beefy arm. He had held him gently—like he had taken obvious care. That said something about him.

Jay led him to an extended cab Dodge Ram. It was huge and red. Fitting. Jay opened the passenger side door for him and waited for Callan to climb inside to close it. Afterward, he stood outside the truck, looking slightly confused. Finally, he shook his head before circling the truck and climbing behind the wheel.

Callan put on his seatbelt. He tried forcing himself to make conversation—like a normal person. "My brother talks about you all the time. You two used to share a room on the road, right?"

Jay flashed him a huge grin. Callan's heart sighed. He was gorgeous in a giant puppy energy kind of way. "Yeah. That's me. I think he said you're some type of artist. Sorry, I don't remember much else."

Callan nodded. "I'm a sequential artist. A comics artist," he clarified, in case Jay didn't know what he meant.

Jay started the truck and pulled from his parking space, following Cato. "Really? I love comics. Have you done anything I would know?"

Callan shrugged, even though Jay wasn't looking at him. "I don't know. Do you read The Villains of Eastland?" Callan went with the most popular comic he illustrated.

Jay's smile was back. "I do. That's you? You're amazing."

Heat filled Callan's cheeks. He dropped his gaze to his lap and fiddled with the sweater he held.

He felt Jay shooting glances his way. "Cato and I have been friends and teammates for years. Why hasn't he wanted me to meet you? I promised him I wouldn't jump or bite."

Callan winced. He was in Jay's truck. Anything could happen to him, but it wasn't in his nature to lie. "I don't think you're the problem." Callan cleared his throat. "He lives in the spotlight. You understand, since you do too. He's just trying to keep me safe." Callan stared at Jay's profile, willing him to understand and not make Callan say the words. To him, the truth felt painfully obvious.

Jay's forehead furrowed. "Why would he think I would hurt you?"

Callan wanted to growl in frustration. "I'm sure he doesn't think that, but people in professional sports are usually pretty rough around the edges. Guys' guys."

"And you're not," Jay said, sounding as if he tried to understand.

"Oh, I definitely am," Callan said under his breath. He swallowed and threw caution to the wind. "I'm gay."

Jay didn't react. At all. He stared straight ahead, watching the road and looking completely relaxed.

Callan went back to nervously fidgeting, buttoning and unbuttoning a single button on his sweater. Finally, he couldn't take it anymore. "So, you like to fight."

A loud laugh burst from Jay at his observation. The sound made Callan smile. Jay looked his way. His eyes shone bright with good humor. "I guess you could say that."

Callan's shoulders relaxed. Jay seemed genuinely nice. He didn't think he had anything to fear. That was a nice change.

CHAPTER TWO

URBAN MIXER TURNED OUT to be a true experience, just as Callan claimed. The ceiling twinkled with stars, mimicking the night sky. Each table was perfectly placed for complete privacy. He spotted more than one celebrity. It seemed a tad fancy for a normal night out for brothers. Of course, Jay's mind latched on to any topic to avoid thinking about his conversation with Callan. He was gay. Obviously, that was no big deal. Jay didn't care about that. He couldn't understand why he couldn't let it go, though. Jay didn't know if he was upset that Cato obviously believed he would be a threat to his twin if he knew the truth, or if it was something else. His emotions were all over the place, keeping him confused. One thing Jay had no doubts about. He couldn't focus on anything but Callan. Jay wasn't the only one.

Their waiter appeared for at least the twentieth time. They hadn't even received anything beyond their drinks yet. He leaned his palm on the back of Callan's chair. "Does anyone need a refill?"

Callan looked uncomfortable as he subtly shifted away from the man crowding his space.

"I think we're good." Cato sounded short. It was obvious Jay wasn't the only one who noticed Callan's discomfort.

The server's gaze dropped to Callan, eyeing him like a feast. "If you're sure I can't get you anything... anything at all."

Callan flashed an uncomfortable smile toward no one in particular.

"We're good." Even Jay heard the bite to his voice.

Callan's gaze locked on him.

Something funny happened to Jay's chest.

The server glanced his way and quickly straightened away from Callan's chair. Jay didn't know what the guy saw in his expression, but he hurried along.

The moment they were alone again, Callan's shoulders visibly relaxed. "Thank you."

Cato stood. "Here. You sit next to Jay. I'll take your seat. If we don't change seats, that guy might plop down in your lap next time he comes around."

Callan popped to his feet. "Thank you." The relief in his voice was palpable.

While they were swapping seats, and no one watched, Jay snagged the chair next to him with his foot. He eased it closer to him.

Callan slid into the chair beside Jay. If he noticed how close they were, he didn't react.

Cato still looked pissed. "Little handsy fucker. We can't go anywhere."

Jay didn't doubt that. Callan had something rare and alluring.

Callan chuckled. "It's okay." Callan patted Jay's leg beneath the table. "Jay can be my buffer now. He's got the size."

Jay swore his chest swelled. Callan made him feel ten feet tall. He nodded. "I've got him."

Cato looked between them. Some of his open ire disappeared. A sheepish smile touched his lips. "Yeah. Okay. Sorry. I guess I get a little overprotective."

"That's what brothers do," Jay said with a shrug.

Callan turned his way. "Do you have any siblings?"

Jay nodded. "I have a sister. She's only five, though. We never lived under the same roof. She was very much a surprise for my mom at forty."

"Where are you from? I detect a fellow southern accent."

He enjoyed having Callan's attention.

Cato jumped in on his behalf. "Jay is a Texas boy."

Jay nodded. "Shady Shores, Texas, to be exact. It's about thirty miles outside Dallas," Jay said before anyone asked. Everyone always asked. "Do you two have any other siblings or is it just y'all? I've never heard Cato mention anyone except for you."

The twins exchanged a glance.

Cato answered. "It's just us. We've only got each other."

The way Cato answered made Jay twice as curious. He didn't dig. Their food arrived, distracting everyone. The server looked slightly irritated when Jay leaned Callan's way and draped his arm across his chair until he left.

Callan looked his way. Their gazes held. A sweet and shy-looking smile touched Callan's lips before he looked away. A strange hunger grew inside Jay. Cato caught his eye. His blank expression gave nothing away. Jay had a bad feeling Cato knew where his mind had gone, though. For whatever reason, Jay liked Callan a little too much. He didn't want their time together to end.

Damn. Jay was so nice. He smelled good and his messy dark hair made Callan want to run his fingers through it. His eyes were this amazing shade of amber whiskey. Nothing about the situation made sense. He highly doubted Jay was gay or even bi. Cato had told him too many stories about women slipping money to hotel workers to let them into Jay's room so when they got to their rooms after their games, the women would be waiting in his bed. Jay didn't always throw them out. He had laughed and groaned over the stories. Now they had met. Callan wished he was brave enough to turn up naked in the man's bed. He was temptation on two legs. Callan couldn't stop blushing every time the man looked at him too closely. It was a conundrum.

"You're right. This is a nice place."

Callan forced himself to hold Jay's stare. "It's my favorite restaurant. I know it's a little too fancy for a Tuesday night dinner, but I don't really go anywhere unless Cato takes me."

Jay shrugged. "I'll give you my number. You can call me if you want to do something. If I'm not on the road, I'm always game to go out. You don't have to eat alone."

Callan cast a glance Cato's way.

Cato's gaze moved between them. He didn't look happy, but he didn't argue. That said something about Jay's character.

He met Jay's stare again. "Okay."

They got out their phones and exchanged information. Callan didn't think he would ever call, but it was nice to think he might have a new friend.

Jay sent him a quick text and then put his phone away. Callan saw the message pop up, but Jay distracted him before he read it. "So do you have any embarrassing Cato stories?"

A surprised laugh burst from Callan. "A ton. Where would you like me to start?"

"Nope. Unh-uh," Cato said immediately, jumping in. "Don't forget this game goes both ways. I have dirt on both of you."

Callan nodded and then looked Jay's way. "This one time in the first grade."

Cato tried coming across the table to cover his mouth. The laughter at the table warmed Callan's chest. It had been a long time since he experienced the feeling of being out with friends. He licked Cato's palm to get him to let go.

"Ewww. Did you lick me?"

Cato shook his hand as if he could shake off the cooties.

Callan laughed harder at his reaction. He cast a glance Jay's way. For a split second, before Jay hid his expression, Callan thought he saw something in Jay's eyes. He shrugged it off because it couldn't be. Still, he spent the rest of dinner thinking about it. It wasn't until they said their goodbyes and Callan climbed into Cato's Hummer that something changed his mind. He checked the message from Jay.

Jay: *See me this weekend.*

Callan drew an unsteady breath. He was more than a little thankful for Cato's loud music covering the sound. His fingers hovered over the buttons. He braced himself. Could he really do this without the buffer of his brother? Before Callan changed his mind, he typed the one word that could doom him.

Callan: *Okay.*

"So, what do you think of Jay?"

The question caught him off guard in an already tense moment. His brain didn't work fast enough. "Uh. He seems nice."

Cato nodded, but kept his eyes on the road. "If I didn't know he was straight, I'd think he was flirting with you all night. But then again, he's always that way."

Callan's insides clenched. He physically fought the urge to be disappointed right on the heels of being asked out. Then again, maybe Jay had meant the offer platonically.

Callan fiddled with his phone. He decided now was as good a time as any. "We're going to do something together this weekend."

Cato shot him a look. It happened too fast for Callan to read him. Cato cleared his throat. "Oh. When did you two decide that?"

They were always honest with each other. "That's the text he sent me at the restaurant. He asked me to do something with him this weekend."

The silence between them was palpable. Callan's nerves were ready to snap. Finally, Cato cleared his throat again. "That's great. You deserve a new friend."

"Yep." A friend. Callan needed a friend. "We'll see, I guess. I'm sure I'll be pretty boring to someone like him."

Silence met his words again. Cato finally broke it. His voice came out soft and low. "Does he know you're gay?"

"I told him on the way to the restaurant. He seemed unbothered."

Cato nodded. "I didn't figure he would care, but you know your safety comes first with me above all things."

"I know." Cato was his protector. Always had been. He was the reason Callan was still alive, no matter how many times their father tried to kill him. Callan was the broken runt who should have died at birth. Now it was Cato and Callan against the world. He knew he owed Cato everything. Still, sometimes he could be a hair overbearing.

"You don't have to worry about me this one time. Jay seems funny, and I'd really like to have a friend."

Cato's shoulders visibly fell. "I know, and Jay is perfect for the job. He's a giant fucking kid, but he'll keep you safe. You know I just worry."

Callan laughed. "That's what two minutes older brothers do."

"Damn straight," Cato growled. "Don't let anyone forget it."

Callan's phone vibrated. He checked it.

Jay: *Great. I'll pick you up at six Saturday night, if that works for you.*

Callan turned his head and stared out the window while he hid a smile. He understood Jay likely only wanted to be friends. It didn't matter. Jay had given him something he hadn't had in a while. He let Callan dream.

CHAPTER THREE

THEIR THURSDAY NIGHT GAME didn't go as well as Tuesday. Jay still had fun. He had been in the box twice tonight. That felt like a low number for him. He supposed since the other team had a leg up on them all night, they weren't as bothered by his chirping.

"Do you want to hit the hotel bar?"

Jay pulled on his shirt and then looked Cato's way at the question. He shrugged.

"Sure. What the fuck else is there to do in Des Moines?"

Cato snorted. "Exactly."

They grabbed their stuff and headed for the bus to take the team back to the hotel. Cato dropped into a seat and Jay took the row behind him. The moment his ass hit the seat, Cato turned sideways and focused on him.

"Can I ask you something?"

Jay had a bad feeling he knew where this was headed, and he had no answers. "Sure."

"What made you ask Callan to do something this weekend?"

Damn. Cato had wasted no time jumping in with both feet. Jay shrugged. "He seems cool, and he said he doesn't get to do much. It seemed like the thing to do. Why?" If Cato could put him on the spot, Jay could do the same.

Cato's gaze skirted away. "No reason, I guess. I suppose I'm just being overprotective. He's not like us."

"What do you mean?" Jay was purposely being obtuse. It bugged him that Cato acted like he couldn't be trusted to hit the town with another grown man, even if that grown man was Cato's brother.

"You know."

Jay blinked. "I guess I don't."

Cato lowered his voice. "You know my brother is gay. I don't want him to get the wrong idea about this weekend."

For a moment, Jay simply stared at Cato while he tried to decide how to respond.

His tongue hit the finish line before his brain. "That's dumb."

"How the fuck do you figure that?"

"Because Callan is an adult. Why are you acting like he has a disability or something? He's a person. Not a sexuality."

Cato growled. "I know that. It's just been my job to keep him safe for so long. I don't know how to be any other way. I just want to know this isn't some kind of game for you."

Jay barely suppressed an eye roll. "This isn't some kind of game for me," Jay repeated back dutifully.

They held each other's stare.

Cato finally nodded. "Okay."

"Okay." Jay tried not to sound childish. For a moment, they ignored each other.

Jay's temper got the best of him. "I think I'll skip the bar. My head is pounding."

Cato shot him an irritated look and turned away. Jay gave in to the eye roll. His gaze moved to the window. He stared at nothing. Honestly, his head actually hurt. His mind hadn't stopped racing since leaving the restaurant Tuesday night. Uncomfortable thoughts had plagued him. Awkward fantasies had sneaked in and set up shop. Even though Jay would take it to his grave, he had watched gay porn for the first time. He constantly fought the urge to text Callan. Jay was furious with himself. He didn't understand why this was happening. He had spent countless hours nude or half nude around other men. Not once had he had strange thoughts about any of them. This confusion drove him insane. A thousand times, he had considered canceling his plans with Callan. Then he would recall how shy and sweet Callan had been. He wanted to see him again. Cato was right to worry.

When the bus reached the hotel, Cato shot to his feet, avoiding Jay. Jay took his time and moved at a slower pace. He stopped by the front desk and asked to have his room checked for unwanted visitors before heading upstairs. It was exhausting but all too common to roust uninvited guests. When he made it to his room, Jay tossed his bag aside and fell face first across the bed. For a few minutes, he simply buried his face in the pillows and tried to clear his head. Callan's smile flashed through his mind.

The memory of Callan touching his thigh made his skin heat.

Jay growled. What the fuck was wrong with him? He dug his phone from his back pocket and rolled. Jay found the messages between Callan and him. His fingers hovered over the screen. He should cancel. Cato was his friend. The way he felt about Callan wasn't right. He was too fucked up over this entire situation. Before he could change his mind, Jay started typing.

Jay: *What are you up to tonight?*

There. He had started the conversation without immediately being the asshole who flaked on their plans.

Callan: *I watched the game and now I'm soaking in a tub full of bubbles. What about you? Are you out drowning the bitter taste of defeat?*

A huge smile stretched Jay's lips. Cheeky fucker.

Jay: *You're supposed to be sad for me.*

Callan: *Okay. Awww, sweetie. I'm so sorry you played distracted and got your ass handed to you. Is that better?*

He was right. Jay didn't lose the game alone, but he had been distracted. Callan had him fucked up.

Callan: *Sorry. I'm used to being honest with Cato. You can tell me to go fuck myself.*

Jay shook himself from his thoughts.

Jay: *No. You're right. I had an off night. It's better now.*

Callan: *Ah. Are you out carousing with the boys?*

Jay: *I'm in my bed in the hotel room, talking to you. FaceTime me.*

Callan: *I'm in the tub.*

Jay: *So?*

He couldn't stop smiling. Even though Jay didn't understand himself, he was happy. That much he knew.

The phone in his hand rang with an incoming FaceTime call. He quickly hit accept. Callan's face appeared on his phone.

"You weren't lying. You are in bed."

Jay's smile grew. His cheeks hurt. "I told you. Why would you think I lied?"

Callan shrugged. His hair was wet and slicked back, leaving his face on display. He was pretty. Jay didn't know how else to describe him. The combination of light blue eyes and a barely visible smattering of freckles across his nose was oddly appealing.

"I've heard stories about you," Callan said, pulling Jay back on topic.

"Like what?"

Callan blushed.

Jay chuckled. Even to his ears, it sounded sensual. "Oh. Those kinds of stories."

Silence swelled between them.

Jay thought about letting him get back to his bath in peace. He opened his mouth to say as much. "Cato is upset with me. He thinks I'm toying with you." Jay blinked. He had not meant to say that.

Callan didn't react. After a moment, he readjusted in the tub, as if getting more comfortable. A wet, bubble-covered hand came into view as he fixed the rolled-up towel behind his head. When he was settled, he finally responded.

"Our dad tried to kill me because I'm gay." The confession froze Jay's lungs. Callan kept talking as if mentioning the weather. "He tried several times, actually. But right after Cato and I turned seventeen and Cato got picked up by the Ice Rockets, he almost succeeded." Callan shifted the phone, bringing his chest into view. There was an obvious bullet wound scar. Callan touched it. "He always wanted a pro career for Cato. Everything he did was to make that dream come true. He hated me for being gay. Dad said I was an embarrassment and Cato would be humiliated by me once he was in the public eye. Everyone expected I would ruin his shot. They thought the Ice Rockets would drop Cato once they found out about me. So Dad shot me, just missing my heart. Cato came unglued. He said I was the only person in the entire family he gave a shit about. As soon as I was healed enough to leave, he brought me with him. We've never looked back. Since then, he's been ridiculously overprotective. So, long story not so short, it's not you. It's me."

Jay didn't know how to feel. Outraged covered quite a few of his emotions, but there was something else simmering beneath the surface he couldn't define.

"Cato is your friend," Callan said before Jay gathered his words. "If you want to forget about this weekend, I'll understand." He didn't sound like he would. In fact, he sounded as if he choked on the words. Jay got it. Cato had all the friends. Who did Callan have?

"No. You're not getting out of this that easily. You said yes and now you're doomed."

Callan laughed. It was a sexy sight. Jay's brain froze at the thought. Had he just thought that? Callan swiped at his eyes. His smile held Jay captivated. Yeah, he had thought that. He wanted Callan. There was no sense in continuing to deny it. Jay knew himself. He was dogged when he wanted something, and he wouldn't stop until he had Callan. Damn the consequences.

Oddly, Callan was having the time of his life. He had expected another boring, lonely night. Now he had this guy he couldn't shake. Callan already knew he would get hurt. Still, he couldn't stop.

"Tell me about this night out that I'm doomed to experience."

"Hmm." The sexy hum made Callan's skin heat. Then Jay smiled, showing off the sexy lines beside his mouth. Callan nearly sighed. "What about the Museum of Contemporary Art?"

"Do you like the museum?" Callan didn't think that sounded like Jay's thing.

"I don't know. I've never been."

Callan snorted. "Don't pick something just because you think I'll enjoy it. Let's do something you'll like."

Jay went back to looking thoughtful.

Callan laughed. "You're really not used to having to take people on dates, are you? You just take them straight to bed." Horror raced through Callan as he realized what he'd said. He rushed to fix it. "Not that this is a date."

"Who said it isn't a date?"

They stared at each other.

Callan's heart raced. He couldn't stop himself from stating the obvious. "Cato says you're straight."

For the first time, Jay looked uncomfortable. "Can I pick you up at ten a.m. instead? I have an idea."

"Sure." Callan would let it go and whatever happened would happen. He wouldn't get his hopes up for anything.

"Good. Bring your swim trunks."

"Swim trunks? Wait. What? It's the middle of winter."

An evil-sounding laugh slipped from Jay's lips. "You heard me. It's supposed to be stupid warm Saturday for this time of year. I want to take full advantage."

"What are we doing?" He honestly didn't care. Callan just enjoyed Jay's childlike joy over keeping a secret.

"You'll see." Jay practically sang the words. "Just be ready for fun."

"I can do that."

They spent another moment simply staring at each other. Even through the phone, Callan felt the heat rising between them.

"I should let you finish your bath."

Callan nodded. "I should let you rest or whatever."

Neither of them said goodbye.

"I'm glad we met."

A smile exploded across Callan's face at Jay's confession. "Me too."

"I'll see you Saturday."

Callan nodded.

"Maybe text me before then if you're bored."

He couldn't stop smiling. "I will."

"Good. Good night."

Butterflies stirred in Callan's stomach. "Good night." He reluctantly ended their FaceTime. Almost all the bubbles disappeared from his bath while Callan stared at nothing, lost in thought. His phone buzzed.

Jay: *Don't forget to send me your address.*

Callan: *I live with Cato.*

Jay: *Sweet. I know where that is. Goodnight again.*

Callan: *Goodnight.*

Callan's cheeks hurt from smiling. He had no idea what was happening, and he still couldn't recall ever being this happy. It had been a long time since he wanted anything this badly. He was scared as hell to be wrong.

Chapter Four

Saturday morning dragged ass to arrive. Callan was a wreck by the time ten a.m. rolled around. When his doorbell rang, he had to stop himself from ripping open the door. Instead, he measured his pace and opened the door like a civilized person. Then there he was. Callan had forgotten how huge he was. He had to tilt his head back to look up at him.

"Hey."

A sigh rose in Callan's throat. He swallowed it before he humiliated himself. "Hey."

That same tension-filled silence grew while they held each other's stare. Finally, Jay shook his head. "Are you ready to go? Do you need to say goodbye to Cato?"

Callan forced his thoughts on track. "Cato is out playing golf." He grabbed the beach bag he had packed and set by the door. "Swimming trunks as ordered."

"Good. Let's hit the road. Fun times ahead."

With a chuckle, Callan stepped outside and pulled the door closed behind him. He had no idea where they were headed, and he still couldn't wait. Once again, Jay opened the passenger-side door for him. Callan climbed in, trying not to feel self-conscious. They were just two friends going out for a fun day. That didn't explain the way Callan couldn't stop eating Jay alive with his stare as Jay circled the truck.

He bounced like a kid as he climbed behind the wheel. "I hope you're ready to get wet."

"I absolutely am." Damn. He needed to reel himself in. He sounded like the thirstiest whore, which wasn't like him at all.

Thankfully, Jay laughed, seemingly oblivious to Callan's undertone.

"Do you plan to give me any hints?"

Jay answered as he pulled from the driveway. "You'll see soon enough."

"Cruel." Callan didn't mean it at all. A strange anticipation rose in his chest. He never got surprises or had fun days. Not really. He watched every road sign, hoping to figure out where they were headed. Callan knew it could be as simple as the beach, or even Jay's backyard pool, if he had one. That still didn't stop him from getting more excited by the second. It felt like they drove forever. They went all the way to Palm Springs.

Callan gawked as Jay headed down the entrance road for an indoor water park. "Oh, my gosh. I've always wanted to go here, but Cato says it's for kids."

"I'm a big kid, so you'll go with me."

Callan fought the urge to clap his hands. He truly couldn't think of a better date or whatever they were doing. The place was slammed, and Callan didn't care. He was more than willing to wait in line. He had seen advertisements for the park. They had water slides and a wave pool for surfing. He was so stinking excited.

"This is amazing," Callan said as Jay opened his door for him. He couldn't hold back his enthusiasm.

Jay kept smiling like he wanted to pat himself on the back. That was fine. Callan did too. He couldn't wait to go zipping down the water slide. Callan practically bounced in place while they waited in line. The line moved. Jay's hand landed on the small of Callan's back as they stepped forward. Callan couldn't focus on anything else. He lost track of time as he focused solely on that hand. Then they were inside the locker room and Callan didn't remember the wait.

Jay found them a locker and peeled off his shirt.

Callan nearly swallowed his tongue. He was solid muscle and goddamn. There were also tons of bruises from the rough and tough way he played.

"Sorry to bother you. Would you sign this gym bag for my son?"

Jay looked toward the guy who approached them. He had a kid with him and a gym bag with the Ice Rockets' logo on it.

Callan hid a smile and looked away, concentrating on changing while Jay got swarmed. He signed bags and took photos with kids. It was adorable. Callan was used to waiting for Cato under similar circumstances.

Finally, Jay untangled himself. He tossed his shirt and shoes in the locker. His gaze moved down Callan's body. "I see you're ready. Sorry about that."

"Don't apologize. You've earned the attention."

Jay's mouth quirked in one corner. "The attention is on you today. It's your fun day."

For a moment, all Callan could do was stare. Everything about Jay was exactly what Callan always dreamed of having in a man someday. He had to force his stupid heart to chill. Callan was still about eighty-five percent certain Jay only saw them as friends. He would make that be enough. It had to be.

Spending the day at the water park with Callan had been one part fun and two parts hell. They had climbed the hill and zipped down the slide so many times, Jay's legs ached. But the way Callan had smiled all day kept Jay going much longer than intended. By the time they made it back to Jay's truck, he was exhausted, and he considered himself to be in damn good shape.

"I don't know how you haven't dropped."

Callan laughed. "Oh, I'll be feeling it tomorrow. I was just having too much fun to stop."

Jay eyed Callan. A slight flush rode on his nose and cheeks. He looked happy.

Something tugged at the center of Jay's chest. He wasn't ready for their time together to end. "Come back to my place. We can order dinner and pick a movie to stream."

Callan shrugged. "Okay. Sounds great."

With a nod, Jay pulled from his parking space and headed home. With every mile that passed, his nervousness grew. Pretty soon, he would know if he really planned to pursue this. If he made a single move, there would be no going back. He wasn't used to lacking in confidence, but he didn't know if he could do this.

"Are you okay?"

Jay looked Callan's way at the question. Concern etched his features. "Yeah, just feeling the overexposure to chlorine."

"Okay. You were looking pretty intense there for a second."

Jay forced himself to laugh. "Nah. I think I just have resting asshole face. Today has been a blast."

"It has. Thank you."

Jay cast another quick look Callan's way. Fuck. He was beautiful. Jay didn't know why Callan had gotten under his skin in a single meeting, but that one dinner together had him so fucked up. Now he couldn't stay away. He didn't want Callan to go home. Jay had to force himself to stick to the topic instead of thinking how soft and tasty Callan's lips looked.

"You don't have to thank me. Believe it or not, no one ever wants to do shit like this with me. Everyone wants to play golf, which I hate. Or they want to have a poker night, which I hate. Even worse, they want to go clubbing, which I hate. I guess I'm a big kid at heart. I still want to go to amusement parks or even just hang out by the pool."

"Well, I'm definitely your man anytime you want to do something like that. I never got to do anything fun as a kid. The entire family's lives revolved around Cato's hockey games. If we traveled, it was for him. If a friend's family invited me to go somewhere with them, my parents couldn't afford to pay my part because every penny went to Cato's hockey. It was fine. All that paid off and I've definitely benefited. I just..." Callan sighed. "Sound like a brat, I suppose."

Jay scoffed. "You sound like a person who deserves things too."

"Maybe." Callan sounded thoughtful. "But now I feel guilty for saying all that."

A small smile touched Jay's lips. Callan was such a good person. It felt good being around him. Jay spent a lot of time surrounded by greedy people looking for a free ride or hoping to win him. For the first time, Jay truly believed he met someone genuine. Maybe that was what he couldn't resist.

That thought held until Jay opened Callan's door and helped him from the tall truck. He didn't want Callan to stumble. Jay didn't give him space. Callan peeked up at him with just the right expression. Jay's hands found Callan's waist. He lifted him from the ground and set him back on the seat again, where they were closer to being eye to eye. Jay shuffled closer until he stood between

Callan's knees. He told himself he had already gone too far. What could a little farther hurt?

He moved slowly, giving Callan plenty of time to stop this madness before it began. Callan's palms slid up his chest. Jay's nipples hardened at the soft touch. Then Callan's arms were around his neck and there was no going back. Jay touched his lips to Callan's. He worried that would be the moment he freaked, except he didn't. Jay bumped his lips against Callan's again. This time, Callan's parted. Jay's tongue curled around Callan's and his dick stirred. In fact, it did more than stir. He went on full alert in a matter of seconds. Jay didn't realize he kneaded Callan's ass until he hauled the guy even closer, as if he could fuck Callan through his clothes.

"You can tell me to stop."

Callan didn't. He kept toying with Jay's tongue, ensuring Jay couldn't turn back.

"Seriously. You should tell me no."

Callan's mouth moved to Jay's neck. He sucked and bit, as if he couldn't get enough of tasting Jay.

Fuck it. He lifted Callan from the truck, leaving him no choice but to wrap his legs around Jay. Jay headed inside and straight for his bedroom. He had no clue what he was doing, but he was doing it. His lust was too far gone.

When he took Callan down on the mattress, and their bodies molded, a bit of reality hit. "I don't want to hurt you."

"Then don't."

Callan tugged at Jay's shirt. He let him have it before doing the same. Jay needed Callan's bare skin against his. There was no slowing, but he still had to be honest.

"I've never been with another man."

Callan nipped at his neck, making Jay pant. "You're doing fine."

That was good enough for Jay. He went straight for the pants. Jay needed Callan nude. He didn't stop feeling frantic until there was nothing between them. Then their bare cocks bumped, and Jay worried he might immediately come. He couldn't recall being this turned on in a long time. Jay had thought life bored him. Now he wondered if he had simply wanted something else.

"This is only our first date," Callan said, sounding a bit mortified as Jay sucked on his neck.

Jay shoved his hand between their bodies and massaged Callan's cock. "No. It's our third."

An exasperated-sounding chuckle burst from Callan. "How do you figure?"

Jay split his attention between exploring Callan's body and easing his concerns. "We had dinner. That was our first date. Then we had a FaceTime date. Date two. So this is three. Damn, I want inside you so fucking bad."

"I hope you have lube."

Jay froze. His mind raced.

"You don't have lube, do you?"

Panic struck. He hadn't thought this far ahead. "Wait." Jay shot from the bed. "I get tested every six months and they always give me this brown bag filled with condoms and stuff, but I've never paid attention to what's inside. Please be lube," Jay pleaded as he found the brown bag stuffed inside a drawer. He opened it and dug through the foil packets. He found three small packets of lube. "Oh, thank God." Jay dropped the bag and tossed the packets on the bed. He opened the bedside drawer and grabbed a condom. "Those cheap-ass condoms they hand out aren't big enough."

Callan's gaze moved to Jay's erection at the claim. "Damn." He swallowed.

"You can still say no."

Callan met his stare. His face was flushed, making his light blue eyes pop. He looked sexy as hell, nude and waiting. "So can you."

A growl rose in Jay's throat at the thought of not having Callan. "Not happening."

"Good."

Jay fell on him like Callan was his last meal. He licked and sucked, incapable of resisting Callan's sexy full lips. Jay wanted to taste them for hours. He equally need-ed to get inside him. Jay blindly rolled on a condom and grabbed for the lube. He ripped into it. His soaked fingers found Callan's asshole. A small part of his brain still kept expecting he would come to his senses. It didn't happen. Jay kept finger-ing Callan's ass like he knew what he was doing. That was how Jay got through life: unfettered cockiness.

"Tell me how to please you."

A ragged breath caressed Jay's ear. "Oh, God. Please don't ask that of me. I get embarrassed easily."

Jay rolled, bringing Callan with him until Callan draped him like the sexiest of blankets. "Then show me. Take what you want." He recaptured Callan's lips so Callan wouldn't feel watched. Plus, he couldn't get enough. It was funny he had never once pictured himself kissing a man. With Callan's perfect tongue curling around his, Jay couldn't imagine ever kissing anyone else again. That was the only part that scared him.

Callan touched his dick.

Jay gasped. He desperately wanted more. This madness was new to him. He usually could get off or not. It didn't matter. It mattered with Callan. He barely contained himself.

Callan positioned himself over Jay's cock. Jay's crown pressed against the tight ring of muscles surrounding Callan's asshole. He didn't know how this could possibly work. Callan seemed so tiny. He moved slowly, easing Jay's meat inside him. Jay ground his back teeth. He wouldn't make it long. Everything was the perfect storm threatening to pull him over the edge. He ached for Callan and his hole felt amazing. This was so new to him, and the excitement gave him a hair trigger. As he looked on, Callan tilted his head back and sucked air as he took all of Jay. The moment Jay's dick fully disappeared inside Callan, he blew. Jay's entire body jerked. He didn't have time to stop it. His body shook as waves of pleasure had him filling the condom. Horror washed over him even as the pleasure rocked his soul.

Callan stared down at him. His heated expression never shifted. There wasn't an ounce of disappointment in his eyes. He looked like he memorized every nuance for a later jack-off session. Callan didn't move. He simply sat on Jay's cock and let him finish.

Jay fought for air, trying to regain function after the powerful orgasm. He wanted more. "Keep going."

Callan didn't question him. He lifted and sank down again. A loud moan tore from Jay like it came from his soul. His dick was hypersensitive. Callan's asshole was amazing. He felt so hot on Jay's cock. Jay needed Callan on the same level as him. He grabbed Callan's erection and tugged, stroking him the way he would himself.

Pressure built for a second time. This time, Jay would hang on if it was the last thing he did. That vow got harder to keep by the second. Callan's asshole was magic.

A small whimper sounded from the back of Callan's throat. That was all the warning Jay got. Cum hit his chest and Jay saw heaven. Callan's ass tried sucking him deeper, and the most powerful orgasm he ever felt sucker-punched him. He held Callan's hips in a death hold and shouted his pleasure. He couldn't stop sucking air as he pumped out every drop.

They were both a gasping mess, clinging to each other and fighting for oxygen. Sweat coated them like they had been at it for hours rather than minutes. Then their lips found each other again. Something shifted inside Jay's chest. This hadn't just been the pure excitement of trying something new. They had a connection. It didn't make sense. He didn't care to find reason in this. Jay liked Callan. He wanted to keep seeing him. This hadn't been a onetime fling. He honestly couldn't wait to see what happened next.

CHAPTER FIVE

CALLAN PLAYED WITH JAY'S fingers and floated on a cloud. Jay's steady heartbeat pounded against his ear. It felt amazing in Jay's arms. He blushed every time he thought about his shamelessness. Callan was not a guy who did things like this. He had leapt on Jay like the horniest of teenagers. Damn. He had blown cum on this sexy chest. Him. He wanted to do it again. Callan had never felt this empowered.

"I guess I should've told you ahead of time about the whole never being with another man thing."

A laugh burst from Callan. "You didn't have to say anything. I knew the moment you showed up on my doorstep wearing cargo shorts in December."

"I have no idea what that means."

Callan laughed harder.

Jay rolled, pinning Callan beneath him as if he meant to make Callan pay for laughing at him. Instead, his eyes softened. "Damn. You really are beautiful."

Callan's laughter died. The air changed. Jay's head lowered. His lips teased Callan's mouth until Callan's lips parted. Then he playfully licked. Callan's breathing deepened. His heart rate kicked up a notch. Something stirred in his chest. He was already too attached and there was no going back. The room slowly darkened as the sun set. Their fingers linked as their tongues played. He felt too much. Callan already knew this would hurt one day very soon. Jay wasn't the one-person type. He wouldn't settle down. Worse, he very much wouldn't want the world to see him as gay in his profession. Callan knew all those things. Still, he didn't stop.

A phone rang nearby.

Jay lifted his head, looking slightly confused. "Oh." He snickered. "I forgot the rest of the world existed." He crawled to the edge of the bed, searching for his phone. Finally, he picked up his cargo shorts and patted the pockets until he found his phone.

He checked the face. "It's Cato." He tapped the phone. "Hello?"

Jay looked his way. "Yeah. He's right here. Hold on." He passed the phone Callan's way.

More than a little confused, he accepted. "Hello?"

"Where in the hell have you been? I've texted you a million times. I thought something bad had happened."

Callan's mind raced. He didn't even know where he had left his phone. "Oh. I forgot my phone in the beach bag. What's up?"

Cato blew out a tired-sounding sigh. "You scared me. I texted to see if you'd be home for dinner tonight before I ordered pizza. Then you didn't respond. So I called, and you didn't answer. Then I texted again, and you didn't answer. So I texted Jay, and he didn't respond. You scared the shit out of me."

Callan winced. "Sorry. We went to a water park and our phones stayed in the locker."

Jay smiled. His eyes danced with laughter.

Callan pulled a "yikes" face. What was he supposed to say? It wasn't a total lie.

"You went to a water park?"

"Yeah, we had a lot of fun." If he only knew.

"Oh, okay. Are you coming home for dinner?"

Jay caressed his cock beneath the covers, making Callan suppress a pant. "You can go ahead and eat without me. It'll probably be a while before I get home."

"Okay. Have fun, I guess."

"I will. Bye." Callan tossed the phone aside. "That was cruel."

The mischievous glint in Jay's eyes got wickeder by the second. "Why? I don't start things I don't intend to finish."

"Then finish it." Fuck. Was that his voice?

Jay crawled closer until he covered Callan's body. His hand found Callan's cock. He stroked as their tongues went back to their earlier play. Callan tried reaching for Jay's dick. Jay shifted positions so he couldn't reach it.

"Nope. This is about you. I want to touch you."

God. His heart. He wouldn't survive this man. For someone who had never been with another man, he was figuring it out fast. He had Callan on fire. All Callan could think about was how Jay had wanted him so badly, he had immediately come. Then he didn't stop. Jay had no idea how that made Callan feel. He had gone so long, living a quiet life so he wouldn't embarrass his brother. Now he had something just for him and it was amazing. No matter how temporary this might be, he was so damn grateful. In no time, he struggled toward release. Even when Jay pulled away and openly stared, watching his every nuance, Callan didn't flinch. He gave Jay the show he hoped to see. Callan writhed beneath his touch. He whispered Jay's name as he came. Most of all, he prayed he was strong enough to handle Jay walking away from him, because he would.

It had been the best day Jay had in a long time. His face hurt from smiling. He swore his soul was satiated in a way it hadn't been in years. Being with Callan was both exhilarating and soothing. He didn't want Callan to go home. Jay kept creating new reasons for him to stay.

"You pick our movie and I'll order the food."

"*Oooh.* What are we eating? I'm starved."

Jay shot him a mischievous look. "Do you trust me to pick something for you?"

Callan shrugged. The shirt he wore belonged to Jay. It was too big and slid down his shoulder at the motion. A different hunger rose inside Jay. He was already addicted. "Of course, I trust you."

Callan's claim pulled him back to the moment. "Excellent." Even Jay heard the childish evil plotting in his tone.

Callan groaned. "Should I be scared? I don't like spicy food."

Jay settled in, ordering way too much food from a hole-in-the-wall hamburger joint most people didn't know existed. "Don't worry. You should only fear being totally turned off by how much I eat."

A bark of laughter burst from Callan. "Don't worry. I live with Cato, remember? I know how much y'all work out and the appetites that go with it."

Jay looked up from his phone and winked. "Exactly. Since you're my current workout, I need to fortify myself."

Callan snorted.

Jay smiled at the sound.

"Well, if I might end up with any type of food, you can watch an animated movie with me. It's probably best you learn I'm a complete child, early in this relationship." Callan snapped his mouth closed, as if he realized what he said.

Jay searched his heart. Was this a relationship? Would it be? He currently couldn't imagine sleeping with anyone else after that amazing experience. Jay tried picturing what would happen if he saw Callan out with someone else. A murderous rage filled his chest. His eye twitched. He would cut that imaginary guy's dick off. Jay needed to clear up any chance of that happening right the fuck now.

"Cartoons are my favorite. For future reference, and since you brought it up, you should also know I'm a horribly jealous bastard who doesn't share."

Callan looked his way. Something flashed in his eyes that made Jay's mouth go dry. "And will I have to share?"

"Absolutely not." Jay made sure Callan heard the seriousness in his tone. He wasn't some teen who planned to ask Callan to go steady or some shit like that, but Callan was his. They needed to establish that.

Callan nodded. "Good."

Jay nodded. "Great."

They held each other's stare. A smile exploded across their faces. Cato would probably never talk to him again. Jay couldn't worry about that right now. For once, he was truly happy. He wouldn't risk its tenuous threads by thinking about reality. Tomorrow would come soon enough. For now, he had found something amazing. He wouldn't lose it.

Chapter Six

Road games were the hardest. Cato still wasn't speaking to him. Jay missed his bed. They were deep in the season, and it looked like they would make the playoffs. Jay was exhausted. He dragged his bag back to the hotel. Then he went in search of the ice machine so he could ice his shoulder. That was where he ended up cornered.

"Hey, Jay."

Jay glanced up at the sound of his name. A blond woman with too much make-up waved at him. She already stood too close.

"Hi." He kept his tone as uninterested as he was.

"Do you need some help with that ice pack?"

He fought an eye roll. "Nah. I'm good."

Her smile grew, making her look a little crazy. "How about just some company, then?"

"Sorry. I'm taken."

She didn't back away. "I won't tell if you won't."

"Yeah. I'll tell. You best believe I'm not fucking up a good thing, but thanks for the offer." He eased past her and slipped back inside his room. Jay took extra care to make sure the door couldn't be opened from the outside. Sometimes fans got a little crazy.

Jay stripped down to his underwear and climbed on the bed with his ice. He stared at the ceiling, willing the pain away. Just a few more hours and he would be home. Technically, he was only a little over a hundred miles away. He could rent a car and be home in two hours. His gaze slid toward the clock. It was eleven. He wondered if Callan was sleeping. Jay dug out his phone. He would text first. If Callan didn't respond, he would go to sleep.

Jay: *You up?*

Three dots danced on his screen immediately, showing Callan typing. Jay's chest felt lighter.

Callan: *Hey. Yeah. How are you feeling? Is your shoulder still bothering you?*

It felt good to have someone care.

Jay: *Yeah. I'm icing it. I feel better talking to you, though.*

Callan: *Oh no. My poor baby. If you were here, I'd kiss it and make it better. I'd baby you until you fell asleep.*

Damn. That sounded nice. Jay bit his bottom lip. Temptation beat him.

Jay: *If I rented a car and drove home tonight, would you meet me there? I know this sounds like an awful booty call or something. I just really miss you.*

Callan: *Absolutely!*

Like that, Jay's pain vanished. He rolled from the bed and started pulling on his clothes. He sent Callan another quick text.

Jay: *I'm leaving now. See you in two hours. If you get there before me, let me know and I'll tell you how to bypass the fingerprint lock and alarm.*

Callan: *Okay. See you soon.*

Jay threw everything together, uncaring if he missed anything. Callan was waiting, and Jay couldn't get to him quickly enough.

Callan sat in Jay's driveway and waited. He didn't know how much longer Jay would be, but he didn't feel comfortable asking him to describe how to bypass everything while driving. Waiting wasn't a problem. Callan just hoped it wasn't a mistake. In a way, Jay was right. This did somewhat feel like a late-night booty call. He couldn't lie to himself, though. It felt good having someone rush home to be with him. His life could be damned lonely.

Headlights pulled in behind him. Callan watched from his side-view mirror as Jay climbed from a too small for him car. A smile stretched his lips. Callan jumped from the car with his overnight bag in tow. He swore Jay brightened like an excited kid the moment he set eyes on Callan. Callan's heart sighed.

"Hey. I told you to call when you got here. You didn't have to wait in the driveway."

Callan shrugged. "It's fine. I just got here like five minutes ago."

Jay closed the distance between them and claimed Callan's lips. Everything inside Callan did a happy dance. Jay pulled away way too soon for Callan.

"Come on. Let's go inside where I can hold you."

That definitely mollified him. "Okay. I want to have a look at that shoulder."

Jay flashed him a smile and took Callan's bag. "Lead the way."

When they reached the door, instead of simply using his fingerprint to get inside, Jay opened a panel beneath the scanner. He typed in a code.

"Set your finger on the scanner until it beeps, then do it five more times until it triple beeps."

Callan followed Jay's instructions.

Jay nodded. "There. Now you'll never have to wait on me. You can just let yourself inside."

Callan had to take a breath. Nothing could have proven more how serious they were becoming.

They headed inside and straight for the bedroom. Jay's house was nice and fit his tax bracket, but it still felt homey. Callan always felt something in his chest when he stepped inside.

Inside the bedroom, they both quietly stripped. They climbed into bed together. Moonlight poured through the window, giving Callan just enough light to see Jay. He eyed Jay's chest and shoulder. Even in the dark, he could see the huge black bruises.

"Shit, baby. I'd tell you to lay off the shoulder checks, but I know you can't."

"It's fine."

Callan shook his head. He knew it wasn't. Jay was just being the tough guy. Callan placed light kisses all over the massive bruise. His body stirred despite his innocent intentions. He heard Jay take a ragged breath. Callan fought the urge to feel if Jay was hard for him.

"I missed you."

Callan's heart soared at the confession. They had only been apart one night, and they were only usually apart for two nights a week. It had been that way since they agreed to be official eight weeks earlier.

"I missed you too." Callan said the words against Jay's skin, being careful not to put too much pressure on his injury.

"Mhmm."

At Jay's hum, Callan's cock grew stiffer. He lightly licked Jay's skin.

Jay's hand found his ass and squeezed. "I'm useless tonight. But if you want to climb aboard, I promise I can still stay hard for you."

Callan's cheeks heated. He couldn't force his mouth to admit his desires aloud. But Callan had no trouble rolling for the bedside table and finding the goods needed to fuck. He rolled a condom down Jay's length.

"Damn, baby. Just your touch makes me hotter than the filthiest of porn."

The heat in Callan's cheeks intensified. He coated the condom with lube.

"I can practically feel you blushing. Sit on my dick. I need that ass."

Callan did as told. He positioned himself over Jay's cock and slowly took him inside. He sucked air. Jay was proportionally sized. His huge cock matched his oversized body. Callan loved it. He hit all the right spots. Callan rocked himself on Jay's dick, taking what he wanted.

Jay's hand found Callan's cock. He stroked. The competing sensations had him gasping for air. "You're all I think about anymore. When I'm on the ice, I wonder if you're watching. If I'm traveling between games, I wonder if you're missing me too. I wonder if you think about me as much as I think about you."

"Yes." Callan meant it as an answer, but it sounded sexual. Jay felt too good inside him.

"You're the best thing that's happened to me in years."

At Jay's confession, Callan went still. He leaned forward and stole a kiss. "You're the best thing that's ever happened to me."

In a flash, Callan found himself on his back, legs in the air, and getting pounded. He held on to the covers beneath him and moaned his way through every thrust. He couldn't think or breathe properly. In no time, pressure climbed his cock.

"Oh, God. Please?" Callan had no idea what he begged for, exactly. He just wanted to come. His entire body tensed. He held his breath. Jay didn't slow. A cry ripped from him as a powerful orgasm slammed into him. His entire body jerked as cum shot from his cock in jets.

"Yes. Fuck. I love it when that ass sucks me dry. Goddamn, Callan. Fuck." Jay growled the last words as he came. Callan couldn't look away. They were amazing together. He never wanted this to end.

CHAPTER SEVEN

JAY NEVER HID HIM. Yet they had been seeing each other for months and still no one had caught on. It was almost funny to Callan. He honestly thought Jay would have to fuck him in the middle of the street before anyone realized they were a couple. Not that he was complaining. People saw Jay as a man's man. Callan understood it might get ugly when people realized the truth. Thankfully, there was likely only one game left in the season.

They stood little chance of making it to the next round of playoffs at this point.

Callan hauled his packed bag down the stairs. He found Cato in the kitchen, standing at the sink with a glass of water. He turned as Callan came into the room.

"Where are you headed?"

Cato was definitely one who should have figured things out by now. Oddly, Callan couldn't bring himself to tell him. He didn't understand why. There was just something off when the topic of Jay arose. "After your team meeting today, Jay and I are flying to Vegas a day early for the next game. After y'all's game tomorrow, we're staying for a while to gamble and whatnot."

Cato nodded. "Sounds fun. You two have been spending a lot of time together."

Callan shrugged. "You spend a lot of time golfing. I never point it out."

"Touché."

They shared a smile.

Callan eyed the clock. "Aren't you supposed to be headed to that meeting?"

Cato checked the time. "Yeah. I was just about to head out. Have fun in Vegas. Don't do anything dumb. I mean, I'll still bail you out if you do, but try to avoid it."

Callan laughed.

Cato gave him a quick hug before heading out. Callan purposely waited ten minutes and then followed. Since Jay had added Callan's fingerprint to his security system, Callan could easily wait for him at his place. They didn't have a lot of time between his meeting and their flight today. Callan needed to be ready to go when Jay got home.

Callan drove the few blocks to Jay's place with a knot in his throat. The feeling came from nowhere and he couldn't explain it. Sometimes reality simply seemed to come from left field. Every day, he grew closer and closer to Jay. Each day, the likelihood of him being completely destroyed got bigger. Jay was on the road a lot. Callan was used to that. He had lived on that schedule with Cato for years. The sporadic being apart he could endure. It was the sure knowledge Jay could have anyone else anytime he chose, Callan couldn't swallow.

He couldn't say why he felt slightly insecure in this relationship. Maybe it was because no one knew about them. Only the fact that Jay didn't hide him saved his sanity. It was also only when they were apart that Callan questioned anything. Jay didn't do anything to make him worry about them. It was just Callan. He had been raised to believe he didn't deserve happiness.

When Callan reached Jay's house, and the garage opened for him, he breathed easier. The moment he set his fingertip on the door leading into the house and it unlocked, the darkness vanished. Jay let Callan have free rein of his home. That had to mean something. As he stepped inside, a smile tugged at his lips. He felt like he was home. A coffee cup from his favorite coffeehouse sat on the kitchen counter next to a muffin and a note.

Hey, baby,

I got your favorite. I'll be home as fast as I can.

-J

Callan sipped the coffee. It was still hot. "Awww." Damn. He had to admit something he couldn't to anyone else. Four months of dating Jay and spending every free moment with him had him so fucking in love. He could never say the words aloud, but they were there. Jay was too much of everything for Callan to resist.

He let himself be distracted for a minute before heading back out to his car. There was only so much time to pull off his joke. Jay truly was a big kid and Callan loved finding new ways to entertain him. He grabbed a hockey stick from his trunk and a craft kit. Callan rushed inside. He gathered all his things, including his coffee and muffin, and settled on the kitchen floor. Callan wanted Jay to see him as soon as he walked through the door. He chuckled to himself as he set to work bedazzling the stick. It didn't matter if he completed the project before Jay got home. He just needed a chunk of it finished for flair.

Two hours later, the back door opened. Jay stepped inside. Callan pasted on his brightest smile and held up the stick.

"Hey, sexy. Look. I found one of your sticks and made it pretty. You should use it tomorrow."

Jay didn't smile the way he hoped. His gaze moved to the stick and back to Callan's face.

Callan's heart dropped. He immediately knew something wasn't right. His throat swelled. He swallowed past the lump. His pulse pounded in his ears. "What's wrong?"

Jay shut the door behind him. He took a breath. "Your brother has been traded to New Orleans."

Callan's heartbeat sped even faster. His mouth went dry. He didn't know what to say or how to react. Callan didn't make enough money to stay in L.A. alone. He couldn't leave Jay. Not yet. He wasn't ready to lose him.

Thankfully, Jay kept talking, saving him from trying to speak. "Cato probably wanted to be the one to tell you, but I couldn't go to Vegas and act like nothing was wrong. I can't spend the next week with you, wondering if you'll choose me."

Callan blinked. "What do you mean?"

Jay made a helpless motion. He didn't move away from the door. It was as if he feared being too close to Callan. "Cato will want you with him. I want you here with me." Jay swallowed. "Like under my roof and in my bed."

Everything inside Callan froze. He was scared to hope. "What are you asking me here?"

"Move in with me. Don't go to New Orleans."

The pounding in Callan's ears kept getting louder by the second. "Why would you want that?"

Jay swallowed again. "Because I'm in love with you."

Callan couldn't breathe. Jay said everything Callan wanted to hear, but things still weren't that simple. "What happens when people finally learn about us? What happens when people see you as gay? Because they will. No matter what you consider your sexuality to be, you'll still only be seen as sleeping with a man."

Jay's features screwed up in confusion. "Who the fuck cares about that? Why are we even talking about that? I'm talking about what matters. If you leave me, it'll kill me. I need to know now if you plan to break me."

Unexpectedly, Callan's eyes filled with tears. "I love you. I could never leave you."

Hope filled Jay's eyes. "Are you serious? You'll move in with me?"

Callan nodded, and Jay was across the room. He pushed everything aside and tackled Callan to the floor.

"Thank god." He kissed Callan.

Callan smiled like an idiot against his lips. Even so, his heart broke for his brother. He had a hard conversation ahead of him, but Callan couldn't leave Jay. For once, he had something just for him. Callan couldn't lose it.

Jay was a complete fucking mess. From the moment the news dropped, he had been ready to fly apart. He had only been dating Callan for four months. Jay knew he shouldn't feel this deeply about them. The thing was, though, he knew himself. There absolutely was a reason Jay had never chased a man before. He was certain he knew that reason: Callan was the one.

They spent every free moment together. Their personalities were eerily similar beyond Jay being a total idiot and Callan being painfully shy. When they were together, those two things disappeared, leaving just them. Jay could not lose this.

Together, they held each other like they weren't on a cold kitchen floor. Jay's insides shook. He had never been as scared as he was the moment he saw himself losing Callan. As long as he lived, he would make sure that nightmare never came true.

Jay reached past Callan and snagged the stick. He held it up to the light and watched it sparkle. "Nice. I doubt it'd pass league inspection."

Callan's body shook with laughter. "It's one of Cato's old sticks. I guess my joke fell flat."

He kissed Callan's forehead. Jay set the stick aside and held Callan closer. "You can bedazzle the whole house if you want."

Callan shook harder, making Jay smile at the silent laughter. "Fuck. We have like ten minutes to decide if we're sticking with our Vegas plans. If you need to go to Cato, I understand."

Callan sat up and grabbed his phone. "Let's leave it up to Cato." He typed on his phone and then waited. The phone buzzed after a few seconds with an incoming text. Callan checked it. "I told Cato I'd heard the news and asked if he wanted me to skip Vegas and come home. He said he's not fit for company, and I should just go and enjoy myself."

Jay watched Callan chew his bottom lip. His heart twisted. "You can go to him. I'll understand."

Callan shook his head. He spent a moment staring into space. Finally, he pushed to his feet. "No. We have a flight to catch, and I doubt Cato will even come home. He'll probably go out drinking with whoever he constantly golfs with. There's no sense in breaking our plans."

Jay rolled to his feet. "If you're sure."

Callan gave him a sharp nod. "I'm sure."

Jay pulled Callan into his arms and stole another kiss. He couldn't get enough. Jay pulled away and pressed his lips to Callan's forehead. He breathed Callan's scent into his lungs. "I love you." It felt amazing finally saying the words that had been haunting him for weeks. He was over the moon when Callan gave them back to him.

"I love you too."

Damn. In so many ways, Jay hadn't expected this. In such a short few months, he already couldn't live without it. Now all he could do was pray Cato didn't say the exact words Callan needed to hear to leave him. Jay still didn't know how much of a chance he stood against the twin who had loved Callan his whole life. It seemed it was time for him to step up his game.

Luckily, Jay was more than accustomed to winning a fight.

Chapter Eight

Callan chose to watch the final game from the comfort of their hotel room. Accompanying Jay would have meant arriving hours early and being stuck at least an hour afterward. Callan much preferred curling up with his snacks and watching from bed. Not to mention, Jay had been chosen—for pure entertainment's sake—to be miked up for the game. His famous chirping antics made for great ratings. Callan was torn between his excitement at watching Jay and being sad about Cato. He knew how much Cato loved the Ice Rockets and California. Callan knew he had to be crushed, but Cato was the type to suffer in silence. Even if Callan had stayed home, Cato wouldn't have bared his heart. There was also the whole dropping of the bomb about Jay thing. Cato would not take him staying behind well. Callan couldn't leave Jay. It was definitely a rock and a hard place. But at the end of the day, Callan had to follow his heart. He had always known Cato and he wouldn't live together forever. Eventually, one of them would meet someone. Callan had just never thought it would be him.

He left the TV running, using the pregame interviews as background noise. Callan was slightly behind on his latest illustrations. Jay had been his sole focus for a while now. But he had a deadline and Callan had to get on it. He drew on his iPad, losing himself in the motions. It was easier to do his illustrations on his computer's drawing pad, but he had to make do.

"Let's go down to the ice where Anna Lively is filling in for Stacey while she's out on maternity leave. How are things looking down there, Anna?'

"Hey guys. Everything looks great from the vantage point. I'm standing here with tonight's hot mic, Jay Ames. I hear you'll be entertaining us tonight."

Jay laughed. "Yeah. I hope they have Johnny on the spot sitting on that censor button tonight."

Callan's head shot up at the sound of Jay's voice. Jay looked sexy as fuck in his full gear. Callan suppressed a sigh. He still couldn't believe they had exchanged I love yous. Jay was a dream come true. Callan kept expecting to wake up. He missed part of the interview due to picturing Jay's body beneath the extensive gear.

"I heard a rumor earlier that you're in a serious relationship now."

A bark of laughter burst from Jay. "Damn, Anna. You never stay on topic."

She laughed. "You know me. I love to be the first at breaking news and the hearts of every eligible female under forty. Do you want to give a shout out to the lucky lady before the puck drops?"

Jay didn't lose an ounce of cool.

Callan thought he might be sick.

Jay released a low laugh. It sounded sultry and wicked. Goosebumps rose on Callan's skin. "Sure. He stayed back at the hotel tonight, but I know he's still cheering for me."

Callan covered his mouth.

Jay winked. "Love you, Callan. See you after I finish kicking these guys' asses."

A hysterical burble of laughter burst from Callan as Jay skated away. His phone immediately rang. Callan glanced down and spotted Cato's name. He declined the call. Callan didn't know what to say. It immediately rang again.

Callan muted the TV and answered. He knew it would be worse if he didn't.

Cato didn't even say hello. "What the fuck, Callan? This is how you let me find out. I'm your goddamn twin."

A nervous laugh escaped Callan. "I don't know what to say. I guess I sort of assumed you would have figured things out by now."

"Fuck's sake." Cato hung up on him.

Callan pinched the spot between his eyes. He honestly didn't understand why Cato was upset. Maybe he thought Callan would ruin Jay's career or recognized Callan would likely not be going to New Orleans. Either way, Callan couldn't fix that now. Instead, he focused on the TV and barely blinked. By the time the puck dropped, Callan's eyes felt itchy from not blinking. He didn't know what this would do to Jay's career, but he feared it might destroy them. Jay didn't know what it was like to be ostracized for his sexuality. Callan did.

Unfortunately, the news must have spread like wildfire. The first time Jay started a fight, the F word immediately flew his way. The station bleeped out the word, but there was no doubt what had been said. Callan flinched.

Jay laughed like he was having the time of his life as he slammed the guy against the glass. Their faces were inches apart as Jay leaned into him, pinning him in place. In a flash, Jay kissed the guy. "Now you have *bleep* germs, *bleep bleep*."

Callan's mouth dropped. A loud laugh burst from him. He covered his mouth again, but the giggles wouldn't stop. Callan couldn't believe Jay had done that.

His laughter grew louder as happiness filled his chest. He recognized something he should have all along. Jay was a kick ass, take no prisoners kind of guy. He didn't play by the rules and gave no fucks. Falling in love with Callan was just another extension of that. They would weather this just fine. Just like with hockey, Jay would love him without bounds. Falling for him had been the best decision Callan had ever made. He would never let him go.

Every muscle Jay possessed ached. He was bruised and sore. They had lost the final game they would play for the season, ending their chances of moving to the next round of the playoffs. While Jay was disappointed, he was tired. He carried his bag inside the hotel, heading straight for the elevator without looking right or left. All Jay wanted was to get back to Callan. He officially had a few months to invest in nothing but them. Jay intended to pour his entire self into Callan. Gloves off now.

He opened the hotel room door to find the room plunged into darkness. Only the light from the TV was left to guide his way. He made it three steps inside the room before Callan leaped from the bathroom. His nude body collided with Jay. Jay forgot everything except the taste of Callan's lips and the bare ass he held.

Callan tried climbing him. Jay helped. He lifted Callan from the floor and headed for the bed.

"Now that's a greeting."

Callan chuckled against his lips. "I love you."

"Mhmm. I love you too, baby."

Jay set Callan on the edge of the bed. "What did I do to deserve this greeting?"

"I just love you. Take off your clothes." Callan sounded breathless. All Jay could do was obey.

He stripped off his shirt. Callan went straight for his pants. Before Jay fully removed his shirt, his dick was in Callan's mouth. He sucked until Jay was rock hard. Jay moaned. His brain stopped working. This was definitely one piece of life he hadn't known he was missing until Callan. Getting head from another man was phenomenal. Still, he didn't want to blow this way, so he eased away from Callan's glorious mouth.

"I want to come inside you."

"Then hurry."

A chuckle burst from Jay at the demand. God, he loved this man. Once he kicked out of his pants, he tried to move away to find the lube.

Callan stopped him. "Don't bother. I've already inserted one of those lube beads."

"Fuck. Every word from your mouth makes me hot. I still need a condom, though."

"Do you?"

It was a fair question. They had decided to move in together. There would be no one else for either of them. They had more than established they were negative and monogamous.

Jay set his knee on the bed.

Callan drew up his knees, offering himself. His asshole leaked lube.

The muscles in Jay's stomach knotted. Callan kept him tied up in his lust. He positioned himself and swiped his cock up and down Callan's crack, teasing his asshole.

A low moan filled the air.

Jay pressed his crown inside.

Callan whimpered as if he couldn't wait.

"Is this what you want?"

"Uh huh."

Jay chuckled. Even to his ears, it sounded wicked. "Then say it."

"I want your dick inside me."

Jay shoved all the way in to the hilt. "Good boy." Callan was getting better at not being as shy during sex. Jay would always love Callan's blush, but he also adored his dirty mouth. He didn't immediately start thrusting. Jay had to hold still for a moment. "Fuck. You feel too good with nothing between us." Jay hadn't been ready. Not one time in his life had he fucked anyone without a condom. Callan always pulled orgasms from him way quicker than he wanted to blow. He used to fuck for hours. Not with Callan. Callan's asshole was witchcraft. Jay didn't stand a chance.

"Give me a second."

Callan whimpered and squirmed beneath him. "Please? I need your cum dripping from me."

Jay saw stars. He forgot everything. His hips moved, taking Callan's ass. The sound of skin slapping skin and grunts filled the room. Jay felt almost inhuman. All he could do was bury himself inside Callan over and over. He needed to come. Jay wanted to watch his jizz leaking from Callan's asshole. He needed to mark Callan as his and his alone.

Callan cried out. His asshole tightened and then sucked, stealing Jay's breath. He exploded. A shout tore from his throat as he filled Callan's ass. His mind turned messy as he became needy. Jay wanted this forever. He needed to know this was permanent. Jay had to know beyond any doubt Callan wouldn't leave him.

"Marry me."

Callan tensed.

Jay stared down at him. He was every bit as surprised as Callan, but he didn't take it back. In fact, he doubled down.

"We're already in Vegas. Marry me."

A ragged-sounding breath escaped Callan. "Okay."

Jay was scared to hope. "Do you mean it?"

Callan nodded. His eyes filled with tears. "Yes."

Jay fell forward and claimed Callan's mouth. He had never been happier in his life. Jay knew things between them had moved at lightning speed from the moment they met. But he swore they were predestined and made just for each other. There was no other explanation for how perfect they were together. Destiny was the only way he could describe how one look at Callan had changed everything about him. He would be the best husband. Callan would see.

It seemed like they kissed for hours. Jay couldn't stop. He stroked Callan's hair and face, savoring every second.

Then he felt a tear hit his hand. Jay pulled away to see Callan's face. Panic hit him at the sight of Callan's tears. "What's wrong? If you don't want to get married, I'll understand. Not really, but I'll still love you. We can wait."

Callan shook his head. "It's not that. I just always thought Cato would be at my side when I married. But he called me earlier, angry I hadn't told him about us. I honestly assumed he had to know. It's not like we've spent any time apart since that first date. But he was upset already about the trade and then he learned about us. He hung up on me and he'll have to move soon. I don't want him to hate me." Callan swiped at his eyes. "Sorry. I didn't mean to turn into a baby."

Jay brushed a kiss across his lips. "No. Don't apologize. Cato is a big part of you. I should've talked to him about us. He's my friend. He should've heard my side. My only excuse is I haven't wanted to take a second away from you for anything else. Between the grueling end of season schedule and everything else, I didn't make the time. I'll call him. You won't lose your brother." He swiped the tears from Callan's face. "I promise. Everything will be okay."

Callan nodded.

Jay tucked him close and held him. He kept placing light kisses on Callan's ear and cheek until he heard Callan's breathing deepen. While Callan slept, Jay stared into the dark and fumed. Cato had been a real asshole lately. It was like he didn't want his brother to be happy. A pang hit Jay in the chest as a thought hit. Maybe Cato truly believed Jay would use Callan and throw him away. Either way, he was still angry. Cato had some explaining to do. As soon as he knew Callan wouldn't wake, Jay would call. He would get to the bottom of this. It was time for Cato to spill.

Cato stared at the fire, watching part of his Ice Rockets' gear burn. He lifted the half empty bottle of Jack to his lips and swallowed. The liquid burned all the way down. Cato couldn't taste it any longer, but that burn was still there. His head spun from the alcohol and his raging thoughts. He was failing in everything he loved.

His performance had been down. It was time for a change. Change benefited everyone. At least, that was the bullshit he had been fed when he got the boot. Cato didn't like change. Callan loved it here. He would stay behind. Cato already felt that in his heart. Callan would choose Jay.

Jay... Cato slid down in his seat and took another drink. That was a whole other story. Cato didn't know where to start. Callan could have anyone, but he had chosen Jay. Everything about that was fucked up. His cellphone rang. Cato ignored it. Unfortunately, it didn't stop. With a growl, he snatched up the device. His lungs froze. It was Jay.

A malicious smile pulled at his lips. So Jay wanted to talk. Fine. They would talk. He answered. "What?"

To his surprise, Jay was ready for his anger. He gave it back to Cato. "What in the actual fuck is wrong with you? I know you got traded and that fucking sucks for a million reasons. But that's no excuse to make your brother cry."

Cato's heart skipped a beat. His eyes immediately stung. "Callan cried?"

"What did you think would happen when he needed your support and you fucking hung up on him?"

The stinging behind Cato's eyes intensified. "Why did it have to be Callan?" Cato couldn't breathe. The words came out in the harshest whisper, echoing the pain in his heart. "You could've chosen anyone, but it had to be my twin."

Jay scoffed. "Dude, are you in love with your twin or something? That's the only reason I can come up with for this insane reaction. He loves me. I love him. Do you think I'm a piece of shit or what?"

A humorless laugh fell from Cato's lips. He had drunk too much. His life was too messed up at the moment. He couldn't stay quiet any longer. "Are you a fucking idiot or just blind? No. I'm not in love with my twin. I'm in love with you, you fucking asshole."

Silence met his confession. The quiet was so thick, he had to check to ensure Jay hadn't hung up on him. Cato took another drink while he waited for the world to explode.

Finally, Jay cleared his throat. "Is that why you stopped spending time with me and started golfing all the time?"

A loud laugh burst from Cato. "I don't even own golf clubs. Can you believe that? Callan hasn't even noticed that part."

"So, what have you been doing?" Jay sounded so serious—like he really cared. That fucked hard with Cato. Jay was amazing. He really was, and it was hell, because Cato wasn't like him. Cato couldn't let himself be who he wanted to be. Fuck what the world thought. He was trapped. But Jay asked, and it was too late to go back.

"I've been fucking a guy who gets paid well to keep his mouth shut." He should have been mortified to say the words aloud. Cato was too drunk and too broken-hearted to care anymore.

Jay blew out a breath. "I don't know what to say."

Cato took another deep swig before responding. "There's nothing to say. I thought you were as straight as they come, and I never had a shot. That was easier. That I could live with because it was just my stupid heart wanting the impossible. Then you fell for Callan, and I knew it. Immediately, I saw it. But I stayed quiet and drowned myself. Knowing it was just me, failing the way I always do, had everything suffering in my life, and now I'm being shipped off to New Orleans while you..." He couldn't finish. It didn't matter. Not anymore.

"What do you want me to tell Callan?"

At the quiet question, panic shot through Cato. He couldn't lose his brother. Cato didn't have anyone else. "Please don't tell him anything. We're the only family either of us has. When I leave for New Orleans, I need him to still think of me as his two minutes older brother who saved him. That's the only good piece of me. Saving him is the only time I didn't fail."

Jay cleared his throat again. "That's not who you are, but I can't make you believe it. Callan isn't your only family. I'm about to be your brother too. Callan and I are getting married tomorrow."

Cato flinched.

Jay didn't stop there. "If you want Callan to still believe in you, then be you. He thinks you hung the moon. Callan has given up his entire life to save your reputation. Be his big brother now. We need a favor, and we also want you here."

Cato cleared his throat. He would never abandon his twin. No matter the personal cost. "What do you need?"

"You're a great two minutes older brother. You know that, right?"

Cato wasn't so sure, so he stayed silent.

"You're also a damn good person and friend. I wouldn't ask you to do this if it wasn't vital."

"It's fine. Whatever you need. I have to take care of my brother."

"Can you grab Callan's important papers and run by my house and grab mine? Then get your ass here to Vegas. Your brother cried over the thought of you not being at his side for this."

Even though Jay couldn't see him, Cato nodded. He thought his chest might explode from the pain. "I can do that." Cato paused. "Jay, I—" Goddamn. He had so much he wanted to say. "Can you act like this didn't happen?"

He swore he heard Jay smile. "Of course. I've always loved you like a brother. Now we really will have that title. As far as

Callan knows, that's exactly what you wanted."

Cato's shoulders sagged. "Thank you. Just text me where to find your papers. I'll be there."

"Thank you. Love you, man."

Cato's throat swelled. "Love you too." It was like knives ripping through his chest. But this was all he would ever have and soon enough he would be nearly two thousand miles away. Then everyone could forget him. Maybe he could forget himself.

Chapter Nine

Callan woke up feeling a mixture of excitement and sadness. He had never done anything this big without his twin. Every milestone of his life, they had reached together. It was odd to have half of himself missing. He still knew he would soon marry the man he loved. That helped a lot. He felt giddy every time he thought about it. Soon he would be Callan Ames. Everyone would know he snagged the most wanted man in hockey. Him. A shy little nobody who just stumbled into the greatest love. It was humbling. The world felt very different now. He knew destiny existed.

He sat on the hotel bed in his white tux and tried steadying his nerves. Jay had worked double time to get them matching tuxes and make everything perfect. He had left to take care of a few last-minute details ten minutes earlier. Soon, they would head downstairs to the hotel chapel. The butterflies in his stomach had butterflies. He knew it was just an exchanging of words and then signing some stuff. Callan's heart knew it was so much more. The hotel room door opened, and Callan's nervousness skyrocketed. To his shock, Cato stepped through the door with Jay on his heels.

"Cato!"

A huge grin stretched Cato's lips.

Jay jogged in a circle around Cato like an overexcited dog. "Cato is here. Cato is here."

Love swelled in Callan's chest. Jay had said he would fix things. Somehow, he had worked a miracle.

"You didn't think I'd miss your wedding, did you?"

Tears welled in Callan's eyes. He was so happy to have his twin with him. Callan shot to his feet and ran into his brother's arms. Cato squeezed him and lifted his feet from the floor, the way he always did. He enjoyed being twice Callan's size a little too much.

Cato pressed his lips to Callan's temple and spoke against his skin in low tones.

"I'm happy for you. I'm sorry if I ever made you feel otherwise. You'll always be my favorite person."

Callan's eyes burned. His gaze found Jay. "Thank you." He mouthed the words for only Jay to see.

Jay winked.

Cato set Callan away. "Okay. Who's ready to get married?"

Callan threw his arms up. "Me!"

Cato laughed at his enthusiasm.

Jay opened the door. "I've been ready. Let's get this show on the road."

On the ride down the elevator, Jay's fingers played with Callan's. Cato stood in front of them, oblivious to the heated looks they kept exchanging. The hotel was huge. It felt like it took forever to reach the chapel. Jay had made them an appointment. It also turned out he had asked for special decorations. They had added purple flowers. Callan's favorite color. In no time, they stood at the altar in front of a man in white and gold robes.

"Who has the rings?"

Cato moved to stand behind them. "That'd be me."

Callan gawked. He hadn't known there would be rings.

Jay smiled like an idiot. He knew he had surprised Callan, and he savored it.

The reverend nodded. "Then let us begin."

Callan half listened to talk of a higher power bringing them together. He stayed lost in Jay's gorgeous eyes. Callan still couldn't believe this was happening.

"Do you, Callan, take Jay to be your lawfully wedded husband for richer and poorer, in sickness and health, from this day forward until you both pass from this life?"

"I do."

Jay smiled like he was being handed the greatest gift.

"Do you, Jay, take Callan to be your lawfully wedded husband for richer or poorer, in sickness and health, from this day forward until you both pass from this life?"

"I do."

Callan smiled so hard, his face hurt.

"Bring forward the rings."

Cato stepped forward and handed them each a ring. Callan flashed his twin a smile as he accepted the gold ring he had never set eyes on before.

"Jay, place the ring on Callan and repeat after me."

Jay did as told. He held Callan's hand.

"With this ring, I thee wed."

"With this ring, I thee wed." Jay's voice shook with emotion as he repeated the words, making tears spring to Callan's eyes.

"And pledge my eternal love."

"And pledge my eternal love."

Callan's lungs stuttered as he tried not to cry. The ring fit perfectly.

"Callan, place the ring on Jay's finger and repeat after me."

Callan held Jay's hand and slid the ring onto his finger.

"With this ring, I thee wed."

Callan's voice shook. "With this ring, I thee wed."

"And pledge my eternal love."

The first tear fell. "And pledge my eternal love."

"I now pronounce you husbands for life. You may kiss to seal your now entwined lives."

Jay hauled Callan into his arms and claimed his mouth. He bent Callan backward, being as over the top as possible. People cheered, shocking Callan so much, he turned his head. Their wedding had gathered a crowd of hotel guests. People held up their phones, obviously recording. They would be on the news in less than five minutes.

"Shit."

Jay laughed at his reaction. "Maybe someone will send us the video."

Cato laughed and hugged them. Callan's heart was full. He couldn't wait to spend the rest of his life with this huge, goofy, wonderful man. Callan couldn't believe he had gotten so lucky.

Jay was over the fucking moon. He hadn't dreamed Callan would actually marry him. Thank God Cato had shown. Jay had barely slept after their conversation. He went over every second they had known each other, searching for any signs. They had spent countless nights sharing the same hotel room and drinking at bars. Jay must've been hella oblivious, because he couldn't recall a single word or gesture that gave away Cato's feelings.

Jay let it go. Cato didn't want Callan to know. He would keep Cato's secret. It was Cato's to share. Jay had an amazing husband now. All was right in his world. They spent the day with Cato, finding a restaurant to celebrate before hitting one of the hotel's clubs. He danced every slow song with Callan, except for the one Callan shared with his twin. Jay's heart swelled watching them together. Despite Cato's confession, he truly loved Cato as a friend, and he was Jay's brother too now. He was proud of the new family he had created.

Cato and Jay both got bombarded with requests for pictures and autographs, but that quickly died as Jay reminded people they were celebrating. Every sports channel and local channel showed clips of their wedding. Everyone knew now he had married his friend and ex-teammate's brother. The fanfare would die down before the next season began. No big deal. All Jay cared about was getting his new husband back in bed and putting the final seal on this deal.

By the time Cato and Callan were giving hugs and saying their goodbyes outside their room, Jay was practically bouncing in place with impatience.

Cato met his gaze. "Congratulations. Really."

Jay nodded. He understood what that cost Cato. "Thank you, and I swear we'll do everything we can to see you as often as possible after the move."

"I appreciate it." Cato kissed Callan's forehead. "I love you. Call if you need anything. You know I'll be there."

Callan squeezed him. "I know. I love you too."

With his head down, Cato walked away. Callan watched him go. Concern etched his features.

Jay took his hand. "He'll be okay. He's still just suffering the blow of getting traded. Once he gets to New Orleans, his competitive nature will kick in again."

Callan flashed him a smile. "I know you're right. It's just hard to see him like this."

Jay tugged Callan into the room. "Come here, Mr. Ames. I'll help you forget."

A bright smile snapped to Callan's lips. "Will you? I'm willing to let you try."

Unexpectedly, pride swelled in Jay's chest. Even just six months ago, Jay couldn't have seen a life like this for himself. Now he would die without it.

"No one is more loved than you."

Callan touched his chest as if moved by Jay's words. "Same."

Jay's mood lightened. He snatched Callan off his feet, making him squeal. "Come here, sexy husband. I want to lick your body."

Laughter bounced from the walls as Jay carried Callan to the bed and tossed him down. Before Callan could get revenge, Jay masterfully divested Callan of his pants.

"What the hell?"

An evil chuckle fell from Jay's lips at Callan's open shock. "Wait until you see my next trick." Jay didn't give him time to guess. He immediately went down on Callan.

Callan's hips left the bed, chasing Jay's mouth. "Oh, God. That's so sexy. I wish I had a picture of this."

Jay nearly choked as a laugh burbled in his throat. Callan was such an open book. He always said whatever thought came to mind. It was one of the many things Jay loved about him.

"Jay."

Callan sounded so serious, saying his name. Jay lifted his head. Callan stroked his face. "I can't stop thanking whichever God gave you to me."

Jay's breath stuttered. His eyes stung. He felt the same. Jay hadn't known what his life had been missing before Callan. Now, he was so fucking humbled by this amazing gift.

Jay crawled up Callan's body, setting his erection free as he went. When he reached Callan's mouth, he teased Callan's lips apart as he clasped both their cocks. Callan moaned against his lips. Jay pleasured them while he explored Callan's mouth. He didn't try to get them there fast. Jay savored making another memory together. When Callan came unglued beneath him, Jay memorized every second. He didn't know what he had done to get so lucky, but he would never take Callan for granted. He was Jay's person. Until the end of time.

Keep an eye out for the next Thin Ice, *Pucked in the Head.*

Please consider leaving a review at the retailer where you purchased this book. Reviews really help with a book's visibility, which allows me to continue writing more stories. Thank you, Charity.

About the Author

CHARITY PARKERSON IS AN award-winning and multi-published author with several companies. Born with no filter from her brain to her mouth, she decided to take this odd quirk and insert it in her characters. One of her greatest loves is writing morally gray characters. You'll find them scattered throughout her hundreds of titles.

*Eight-time Readers' Favorite Award Winner

*2015 Passionate Plume Award Finalist

*2013 Reviewers' Choice Award Winner

*2012 ARRA Finalist for Favorite Paranormal Romance

*Five-time winner of The Mistress of the Darkpath

Connect with her online:

*Sign up for her newsletter: https://sendfox.com/charityparkerson

*Join her readers' group on Facebook: http://bit.ly/CharitysTribe

*Website: https://www.charityparkerson.com

*A list of her social media accounts and giveaways all in one place: http://hy.page/charityparkerson

www.ingramcontent.com/pod-product-compliance
Lightning Source LLC
Chambersburg PA
CBHW060350180626
46817CB00008B/2962